'TIME IS A
CATASTROPHE,
PERPETUAL AND
IRREVERSIBLE.'

ITALO CALVINO
Born 1923, Santiago de las Vegas, Cuba
Died 1985, Siena, Italy

'The Distance of the Moon' and 'Without Colours' were
originally published in *Cosmicomics* (*Le Cosmicomiche*) in 1965.
'As Long as the Sun Lasts' was first published in *World Memory
and Other Cosmicomic Stories* (*La memoria del mondo e alter storie
cosmicomiche*) in 1968. 'Implosion' is taken from *The Complete
Cosmicomics*, published in 2009.

ITALO CALVINO

The Distance of the Moon

*Translated by Martin McLaughlin,
Tim Parks and William Weaver*

PENGUIN BOOKS

PENGUIN CLASSICS

UK | USA | Canada | Ireland | Australia
India | New Zealand | South Africa

Penguin Books is part of the Penguin Random House group
of companies whose addresses can be found at
global.penguinrandomhouse.com.

First published in Penguin Classics 2009
This edition first published 2018

012

Set in 11.2/13.75 pt Dante MT Std
Typeset by Jouve (UK), Milton Keynes
Printed and bound in Great Britain by Clays Ltd, Elcograf S.p.A.

ISBN: 978-0-241-33910-7

Contents

The Distance of the Moon

At one time, according to Sir George H. Darwin, the Moon was very close to the Earth. Then the tides gradually pushed her far away: the tides that the Moon herself causes in the Earth's waters, where the Earth slowly loses energy.

How well I know! – *old Qfwfq cried* – the rest of you can't remember, but I can. We had her on top of us all the time, that enormous Moon: when she was full – nights as bright as day, but with a butter-coloured light – it looked as if she were going to crush us; when she was new, she rolled around the sky like a black umbrella blown by the wind; and when she was waxing, she came forward with her horns so low she seemed about to stick into the peak of a promontory and get caught there. But the whole business of the Moon's phases worked in a different way then: because the distances from the Sun were different, and the orbits, and the angle of something or other, I forget what; as for eclipses, with Earth and Moon stuck together the way they were, why, we had eclipses every minute: naturally, those two big monsters managed to put each other in the shade constantly, first one, then the other.

Orbit? Oh, elliptical, of course: for a while it would huddle against us and then it would take flight for a while. The tides, when the Moon swung closer, rose so high nobody could hold them back. There were nights when the Moon was full and very, very low, and the tide was so high that the Moon missed a ducking in the sea by a hair's breadth; well, let's say a few yards anyway. Climb up on the Moon? Of course we did. All you had to do was row out to it in a boat and, when you were underneath, prop a ladder against her and scramble up.

The spot where the Moon was lowest, as she went by, was off the Zinc Cliffs. We used to go out with those little rowing boats they had in those days, round and flat, made of cork. They held quite a few of us: me, Captain Vhd Vhd, his wife, my deaf cousin, and sometimes little Xlthlx – she was twelve or so at that time. On those nights the water was very calm, so silvery it looked like mercury, and the fish in it, violet-coloured, unable to resist the Moon's attraction, rose to the surface, all of them, and so did the octopuses and the saffron medusas. There was always a flight of tiny creatures – little crabs, squid, and even some weeds, light and filmy, and coral plants – that broke from the sea and ended up on the

Moon, hanging down from that lime-white ceiling, or else they stayed in mid-air, a phosphorescent swarm we had to drive off, waving banana leaves at them.

This is how we did the job: in the boat we had a ladder: one of us held it, another climbed to the top, and a third, at the oars, rowed until we were right under the Moon; that's why there had to be so many of us (I only mentioned the main ones). The man at the top of the ladder, as the boat approached the Moon, would become scared and start shouting: 'Stop! Stop! I'm going to bang my head!' That was the impression you had, seeing her on top of you, immense, and all rough with sharp spikes and jagged, saw-tooth edges. It may be different now, but then the Moon, or rather the bottom, the underbelly of the Moon, the part that passed closest to the Earth and almost scraped it, was covered with a crust of sharp scales. It had come to resemble the belly of a fish, and the smell too, as I recall, if not downright fishy, was faintly similar, like smoked salmon.

In reality, from the top of the ladder, standing erect on the last rung, you could just touch the Moon if you held your arms up. We had taken the measurements carefully (we didn't yet suspect that she was moving away from us); the only thing you had to be very careful about was where you put your hands. I always chose a scale that seemed fast (we climbed up in groups of five or six at a time), then I would cling first with one hand, then with both, and immediately I would feel ladder and boat drifting away from below me, and the motion of the Moon would tear me from the Earth's attraction. Yes, the Moon was so strong that she pulled you up; you realized this the moment you passed from one to the other: you had to swing up abruptly, with a kind of somersault, grabbing the scales, throwing your legs over your head, until your feet were on the Moon's surface. Seen from the Earth, you looked as if you were hanging there with your head down, but for you, it was the normal position, and the only odd thing was that when you raised your eyes you saw the sea above you, glistening, with the boat and the others upside down, hanging like a bunch of grapes from the vine.

My cousin, the Deaf One, showed a special talent for making those leaps. His clumsy hands, as soon as they touched the lunar surface (he was always the first to jump up from the ladder), suddenly became deft and sensitive. They found immediately the spot where he could hoist himself up; in fact just the pressure of his palms seemed enough to make him stick to the satellite's crust. Once I even thought I saw the Moon come towards him, as he held out his hands.

He was just as dextrous in coming back down to Earth, an operation still more difficult. For us, it consisted in jumping, as high as we could, our arms upraised (seen from the Moon, that is, because seen from the Earth it looked more like a dive, or like swimming downwards, arms at our sides), like jumping up from the Earth in other words, only now we were without the ladder, because there was nothing to prop it against on the Moon. But instead of jumping with his arms out, my cousin bent towards the Moon's surface, his head down as if for a somersault, then made a leap, pushing with his hands. From the boat we watched him, erect in the air as if he were supporting the Moon's enormous ball and were tossing it, striking it with his palms; then, when his legs came within reach, we managed to grab his ankles and pull him down on board.

Now, you will ask me what in the world we went up on the Moon for; I'll explain it to you. We went to collect the milk, with a big spoon and a bucket. Moon-milk was very thick, like a kind of cream cheese. It formed in the crevices between one scale and the next, through the fermentation of various bodies and substances of terrestrial origin which had flown up from the prairies and forests and lakes, as the Moon sailed over them. It was composed chiefly of vegetal juices, tadpoles, bitumen, lentils, honey, starch crystals, sturgeon eggs, moulds, pollens, gelatinous matter, worms, resins, pepper, mineral salts, combustion residue. You had only to dip the spoon under the scales that covered the Moon's scabby terrain, and you brought it out filled with that precious muck. Not in the pure state, obviously; there was a lot of refuse. In the fermentation (which took place as the Moon passed over the expanses of hot air above the deserts) not all the bodies melted; some remained stuck in it: finger-nails and cartilage, bolts, sea horses, nuts and peduncles, shards of crockery, fish-hooks, at times even a comb. So this paste, after it was collected, had to be refined, fil-tered. But that wasn't the difficulty: the hard part was transporting it down to the Earth. This is how we did it: we hurled each spoonful into the air with both hands, using the spoon as a catapult. The cheese flew, and if we had thrown it hard enough, it stuck to the ceiling, I mean the surface of the sea. Once there, it floated, and it was easy enough to pull it into the boat. In this operation, too, my deaf cousin displayed a special gift; he had strength and a good aim; with a single, sharp throw, he could send the cheese straight into a bucket we held up to him from the boat. As for me, I occasionally misfired; the contents of the spoon would fail to overcome the Moon's attraction and they would fall back into my eye.

I still haven't told you everything about the things my cousin was good at. That job of extracting lunar milk from the Moon's scales was child's play to him: instead of the spoon, at times he had only to thrust his bare hand under the scales, or even one finger. He didn't proceed in any orderly way, but went to isolated places, jumping from one to the other, as if he were playing tricks on the Moon, surprising her, or perhaps tickling her. And wherever he put his hand, the milk spurted out as if from a nanny goat's teats. So the rest of us had only to follow him and collect with our spoons the substance that he was pressing out, first here, then there, but always as if by chance, since the Deaf One's movements seemed to have no clear, practical sense. There were places, for example, that he touched merely for the fun of touching them: gaps between two scales, naked and tender folds of lunar flesh. At times my cousin pressed not only his fingers but – in a carefully gauged leap – his big toe (he climbed on to the Moon barefoot) and this seemed to be the height of amusement for him, if we could judge by the chirping sounds that came from his throat as he went on leaping.

The soil of the Moon was not uniformly scaly, but revealed irregular bare patches of pale, slippery clay. These soft areas inspired the Deaf One to turn somersaults or to fly almost like a bird, as if he wanted to impress his whole body into the Moon's pulp. As he ventured further in this way, we lost sight of him at one point. On the Moon there were vast areas we had never had any reason or curiosity to explore, and that was where my cousin vanished; I had suspected that all those somersaults and nudges he indulged in before our eyes were only a preparation, a prelude to something secret meant to take place in the hidden zones.

We fell into a special mood on those nights off the Zinc Cliffs: gay, but with a touch of suspense, as if inside our skulls, instead of the brain, we felt a fish, floating, attracted by the Moon. And so we navigated, playing and singing. The Captain's wife played the harp; she had very long arms, silvery as eels on those nights, and armpits as dark and mysterious as sea urchins; and the sound of the harp was sweet and piercing, so sweet and piercing it was almost unbearable, and we were forced to let out long cries, not so much to accompany the music as to protect our hearing from it.

Transparent medusas rose to the sea's surface, throbbed there a moment, then flew off, swaying towards the Moon. Little Xlthlx amused herself by catching them in midair, though it wasn't easy. Once, as she stretched her little arms out to catch one, she jumped up slightly and was also set free. Thin as she was, she was an ounce or two short of the weight necessary for the Earth's gravity to overcome the Moon's attraction and bring her back: so she flew up among the medusas, suspended over the sea. She took fright, cried, then laughed and started playing, catching shellfish and minnows as they flew, sticking some into her mouth and chewing them. We rowed hard, to keep up with the child: the Moon ran off in her ellipse, dragging that swarm of marine fauna through the sky, and a train of long, entwined seaweeds, and Xlthlx hanging there in the midst. Her two wispy braids seemed to be flying on their own, outstretched towards the Moon; but all the while she kept wriggling and kicking at the air, as if she wanted to fight that influence, and her socks – she had lost her shoes in the fight – slipped off her feet and swayed, attracted by the Earth's force. On the ladder, we tried to grab them.

The idea of eating the little animals in the air had been a good one; the more weight Xlthlx gained, the more she sank towards the Earth; in fact, since among those hovering bodies hers was the largest, molluscs and seaweeds and plankton began to gravitate about her, and soon the child was covered with siliceous little shells, chitinous carapaces and fibres of sea plants. And the further she vanished into that tangle, the more she was freed of the Moon's influence, until she grazed the surface of the water and sank into the sea.

We rowed quickly, to pull her out and save her: her body had remained magnetized, and we had to work hard to scrape off all the things encrusted on her. Tender corals were wound about her head, and every time we ran the comb through her hair there was a shower of crayfish and sardines; her eyes were sealed shut by limpets clinging to the lids with their suckers; squids' tentacles were coiled around her arms and her neck; and her little dress now seemed woven only of weeds and sponges. We got the worst of it off her, but for weeks afterwards she went on pulling out fins and shells, and her skin, dotted with little diatoms, remained affected for ever, looking – to someone who didn't observe her carefully – as if it were faintly dusted with freckles.

This should give you an idea of how the influences of Earth and Moon, practically equal, fought over the space between them. I'll tell you something else: a body that descended to the Earth from the satellite was still charged for a while with lunar force and rejected the attraction of our world. Even I, big and heavy as I was: every time I had been up there, I took a while to get used to the Earth's up and its down, and the others would have to grab my arms and hold me, clinging in a bunch in the swaying boat while I still had my head hanging and my legs stretching up towards the sky.

'Hold on! Hold on to us!' they shouted at me, and in all that groping, sometimes I ended up by seizing one of Mrs Vhd Vhd's breasts, which were round and firm and the contact was good and secure and had an attraction as strong as the Moon's or even stronger, especially if I managed, as I plunged down, to put my other arm around her hips, and with this I passed back into our world and fell with a thud into the bottom of the boat, where Captain Vhd Vhd brought me around, throwing a bucket of water in my face.

This is how the story of my love for the Captain's wife began, and my suffering. Because it didn't take me long to realize whom the lady kept looking at insistently: when my cousin's hands clasped the satellite, I watched Mrs Vhd Vhd, and in her eyes I could read the thoughts that the deaf man's familiarity with the Moon were arousing in her; and when he disappeared in his mysterious lunar explorations, I saw her become restless, as if on pins and needles, and then it was all clear to me, how Mrs Vhd Vhd was becoming jealous of the Moon and I was jealous of my cousin. Her eyes were made of diamonds, Mrs Vhd Vhd's; they flared when she looked at the Moon, almost challengingly, as if she were saying: 'You shan't have him!' And I felt like an outsider.

The one who least understood all of this was my deaf cousin. When we helped him down, pulling him – as I explained to you – by his legs, Mrs Vhd Vhd lost all her self-control, doing everything she could to take his weight against her own body, folding her long silvery arms around him; I felt a pang in my heart (the times I clung to her, her body was soft and kind, but not thrust forward, the way it was with my cousin), while he was indifferent, still lost in his lunar bliss.

I looked at the Captain, wondering if he also noticed his wife's behaviour; but there was never a trace of any expression on that face of his, eaten by brine, marked with tarry wrinkles. Since the Deaf One was always the last to break away from the Moon, his return was the signal for the boats to move off. Then, with an unusually polite gesture, Vhd Vhd picked up the harp from the bottom of the boat and handed it to his wife. She was obliged to take it and play a few notes. Nothing could separate her more from the Deaf One than the sound of the harp. I took to singing in a low voice that sad song that goes: 'Every shiny fish is floating, floating; and every dark fish is at the bottom, at the bottom of the sea . . .' and all the others, except my cousin, echoed my words.

Every month, once the satellite had moved on, the Deaf One returned to his solitary detachment from the things of the world; only the approach of the full moon aroused him again. That time I had arranged things so it wasn't my turn to go up, I could stay in the boat with the Captain's wife. But then, as soon as my cousin had climbed the ladder, Mrs Vhd Vhd said: 'This time I want to go up there, too!'

This had never happened before; the Captain's wife had never gone up on the Moon. But Vhd Vhd made no objection, in fact he almost pushed her up the ladder bodily, exclaiming: 'Go ahead then!' and we all started helping her, and I held her from behind, felt her round and soft on my arms, and to hold her up I began to press my face and the palms of my hands against her, and when I felt her rising into the Moon's sphere I was heartsick at that lost contact, so I started to rush after her, saying: 'I'm going to go up for a while, too, to help out!'

I was held back as if in a vice. 'You stay here; you have work to do later,' the Captain commanded, without raising his voice.

At that moment each one's intentions were already clear. And yet I couldn't figure things out; even now I'm not sure I've interpreted it all correctly. Certainly the Captain's wife had for a long time been cherishing the desire to go off privately with my cousin up there (or at least to prevent him from going off alone with the Moon), but probably she had a still more ambitious plan, one that would have to be carried out in agreement with the Deaf One: she wanted the two of them to hide up there together and stay on the Moon for a month. But perhaps my cousin, deaf as he was, hadn't understood anything of what she had tried to explain to him, or perhaps he hadn't even realized that he was the object of the lady's desires. And the Captain? He wanted nothing better than to be rid of his wife; in fact, as soon as she was confined up there, we saw him give free rein to his inclinations and plunge into vice, and then we understood why he had done nothing to hold her back. But had he known from the beginning that the Moon's orbit was widening?

None of us could have suspected it. The Deaf One perhaps, but only he: in the shadowy way he knew things, he may have had a presentiment that he would be forced to bid the Moon farewell that night. This is why he hid in his secret places and reappeared only when it was time to come back down on board. It was no use for the Captain's wife to try to follow him: we saw her cross the scaly zone various times, length and breadth, then suddenly she stopped, looking at us in the boat, as if about to ask us whether we had seen him.

Surely there was something strange about that night. The sea's surface, instead of being taut as it was during the full moon, or even arched a bit towards the sky, now seemed limp, sagging, as if the lunar magnet no longer exercised its full power. And the light, too, wasn't the same as the light of other full moons; the night's shadows seemed somehow to have thickened. Our friends up there must have realized what was happening; in fact, they looked up at us with frightened eyes. And from their mouths and ours, at the same moment, came a cry: 'The Moon's going away!'

The cry hadn't died out when my cousin appeared on the Moon, running. He didn't seem frightened, or even amazed: he placed his hands on the terrain, flinging himself into his usual somersault, but this time after he had hurled himself into the air he remained suspended, as little Xlthlx had. He hovered a moment between Moon and Earth, upside down, then laboriously moving his arms, like someone swimming against a current, he headed with unusual slowness towards our planet.

From the Moon the other sailors hastened to follow his example. Nobody gave a thought to getting the Moon-milk that had been collected into the boats, nor did the Captain scold them for this. They had already waited too long, the distance was difficult to cross by now; when they tried to imitate my cousin's leap or his swimming, they remained there groping, suspended in mid-air. 'Cling together! Idiots! Cling together!' the Captain yelled. At this command, the sailors tried to form a group, a mass, to push all together until they reached the zone of the Earth's attraction: all of a sudden a cascade of bodies plunged into the sea with a loud splash.

The boats were now rowing to pick them up. 'Wait! The Captain's wife is missing!' I shouted. The Captain's wife had also tried to jump, but she was still floating only a few yards from the Moon, slowly moving her long, silvery arms in the air. I climbed up the ladder, and in a vain attempt to give her something to grasp I held the harp out towards her. 'I can't reach her! We have to go after her!' and I started to jump up, brandishing the harp. Above me the enormous lunar disc no longer seemed the same as before: it had become much smaller, it kept contracting, as if my gaze were driving it away, and the emptied sky gaped like an abyss where, at the bottom, the stars had begun multiplying, and the night poured a river of emptiness over me, drowned me in dizziness and alarm.

'I'm afraid,' I thought. 'I'm too afraid to jump. I'm a coward!' and at that moment I jumped. I swam furiously through the sky, and held the harp out to her, and instead of coming towards me she rolled over and over, showing me first her impassive face and then her backside.

'Hold tight to me!' I shouted, and I was already over-taking her, entwining my limbs with hers. 'If we cling together we can go down!' and I was concentrating all my strength on uniting myself more closely with her, and I concentrated my sensations as I enjoyed the full-ness of that embrace. I was so absorbed I didn't realize at first that I was, indeed, tearing her from her weightless condition, but was making her fall back on the Moon. Didn't I realize it? Or had that been my intention from the very beginning? Before I could think properly, a cry was already bursting from my throat. 'I'll be the one to stay with you for a month!' Or rather, 'On you!' I shouted, in my excitement: 'On you for a month!' and at that moment our embrace was broken by our fall to the Moon's surface, where we rolled away from each other among those cold scales.

I raised my eyes as I did every time I touched the Moon's crust, sure that I would see above me the native sea like an endless ceiling, and I saw it, yes, I saw it this time, too, but much higher, and much more narrow, bound by its borders of coasts and cliffs and promontories, and how small the boats seemed, and how unfamiliar my friends' faces and how weak their cries! A sound reached me from nearby: Mrs Vhd Vhd had discovered her harp and was caressing it, sketching out a chord as sad as weeping.

A long month began. The Moon turned slowly around the Earth. On the suspended globe we no longer saw our familiar shore, but the passage of oceans as deep as abysses and deserts of glowing lapilli, and continents of ice, and forests writhing with reptiles, and the rocky walls of mountain chains gashed by swift rivers, and swampy cities, and stone graveyards, and empires of clay and mud. The distance spread a uniform colour over everything: the alien perspectives made every image alien; herds of elephants and swarms of locusts ran over the plains, so evenly vast and dense and thickly grown that there was no difference among them.

I should have been happy: as I had dreamed, I was

alone with her, that intimacy with the Moon I had so often envied my cousin and with Mrs Vhd Vhd was now my exclusive prerogative, a month of days and lunar nights stretched uninterrupted before us, the crust of the satellite nourished us with its milk, whose tart flavour was familiar to us, we raised our eyes up, up to the world where we had been born, finally traversed in all its various expanse, explored landscapes no Earth-being had ever seen, or else we contemplated the stars beyond the Moon, big as pieces of fruit, made of light, ripened on the curved branches of the sky, and everything exceeded my most luminous hopes, and yet, and yet, it was, instead, exile.

I thought only of the Earth. It was the Earth that caused each of us to be that someone he was rather than someone else; up there, wrested from the Earth, it was as if I were no longer that I, nor she that She, for me. I was eager to return to the Earth, and I trembled at the fear of having lost it. The fulfilment of my dream of love had lasted only that instant when we had been united, spinning between Earth and Moon; torn from its earthly soil, my love now knew only the heart-rending nostalgia for what it lacked: a where, a surrounding, a before, an after.

This is what I was feeling. But she? As I asked myself, I was torn by my fears. Because if she also thought only of the Earth, this could be a good sign, a sign that she had finally come to understand me, but it could also mean that everything had been useless, that her longings were directed still and only towards my deaf cousin. Instead, she felt nothing. She never raised her eyes to the old planet, she went off, pale, among those wastelands, mumbling dirges and stroking her harp, as if completely identified with her temporary (as I thought) lunar state. Did this mean I had won out over my rival? No; I had lost: a hopeless defeat. Because she had finally realized that my cousin loved only the Moon, and the only thing she wanted now was to become the Moon, to be assimilated into the object of that extrahuman love.

When the Moon had completed its circling of the planet, there we were again over the Zinc Cliffs. I recognized them with dismay: not even in my darkest previsions had I thought the distance would have made them so tiny. In that mud puddle of the sea, my friends had set forth again, without the now-useless ladders; but from the boats rose a kind of forest of long poles; everybody was brandishing one, with a harpoon or a grappling hook at the end, perhaps in the hope of scraping off a last bit of Moon-milk or of lending some kind of help to us wretches up there. But it was soon clear that no pole was long enough to reach the Moon; and they dropped back, ridiculously short, humbled, floating on the sea; and in that confusion some of the boats were thrown off balance and overturned. But just then, from another vessel a longer pole, which till then they had dragged along on the water's surface, began to rise: it must have been made of bamboo, of many, many bamboo poles stuck one into the other, and to raise it they had to go slowly because – thin as it was – if they let it sway too much it might break. Therefore, they had to use it with great strength and skill, so that the wholly vertical weight wouldn't rock the boat.

Suddenly it was clear that the tip of that pole would touch the Moon, and we saw it graze, then press against the scaly terrain, rest there a moment, give a kind of little push, or rather a strong push that made it bounce off again, then come back and strike that same spot as if on the rebound, then move away once more. And I recognized, we both – the Captain's wife and I – recognized my cousin: it couldn't have been anyone else, he was playing his last game with the Moon, one of his tricks, with the Moon on the tip of his pole as if he were juggling with her. And we realized that his virtuosity had no purpose, aimed at no practical result, indeed you would have said he was driving the Moon away, that he was helping her departure, that he wanted to show her to her more distant orbit. And this, too, was just like him: he was unable to conceive desires that went against the Moon's nature, the Moon's course and destiny, and if the

Moon now tended to go away from him, then he would take delight in this separation just as, till now, he had delighted in the Moon's nearness.

What could Mrs Vhd Vhd do, in the face of this? It was only at this moment that she proved her passion for the deaf man hadn't been a frivolous whim but an irrevocable vow. If what my cousin now loved was the distant Moon, then she too would remain distant, on the Moon. I sensed this, seeing that she didn't take a step towards the bamboo pole, but simply turned her harp towards the Earth, high in the sky, and plucked the strings. I say I saw her, but to tell the truth I only caught a glimpse of her out of the corner of my eye, because the minute the pole had touched the lunar crust, I had sprung and grasped it, and now, fast as a snake, I was climbing up the bamboo knots, pushing myself along with jerks of my arms and knees, light in the rarefied space, driven by a natural power that ordered me to return to the Earth, oblivious of the motive that had brought me here, or perhaps more aware of it than ever and of its unfortunate outcome; and already my climb up the swaying pole had reached the point where I no longer had to make any effort but could just allow myself to slide, head first, attracted by the Earth, until in my haste the pole broke into a thousand pieces and I fell into the sea, among the boats.

My return was sweet, my home refound, but my thoughts were filled only with grief at having lost her, and my eyes gazed at the Moon, for ever beyond my reach, as I sought her. And I saw her. She was there where I had left her, lying on a beach directly over our heads, and she said nothing. She was the colour of the Moon; she held the harp at her side and moved one hand now and then in slow arpeggios. I could distinguish the shape of her bosom, her arms, her thighs, just as I remember them now, just as now, when the Moon has become that flat, remote circle, I still look for her as soon as the first silver appears in the sky, and the more it waxes, the more clearly I imagine I can see her, her or something of her, but only her, in a hundred, a thousand different vistas, she who makes the Moon the Moon and, whenever she is full, sets the dogs to howling all night long, and me with them.

Without Colours

*Before forming its atmosphere and its oceans, the Earth must
have resembled a grey ball revolving in space. As the Moon does
now; where the ultraviolet rays radiated by the Sun arrive
directly, all colours are destroyed, which is why the cliffs of the
lunar surface, instead of being coloured like Earth's, are of a
dead, uniform grey. If the Earth displays a varicoloured coun-
tenance, it is thanks to the atmosphere, which filters that
murderous light.*

A bit monotonous – *Qfwfq confirmed* – but restful, all the
same. I could go for miles and miles at top speed, the
way you can move where there isn't any air about, and
all I could see was grey upon grey. No sharp contrasts:
the only really white white, if there was any, lay in the
centre of the Sun and you couldn't even begin to approach it with your eyes; and as far as really black black is
concerned, there wasn't even the darkness of night,
because all the stars were constantly visible. Uninterrupted horizons opened before me with mountain

chains just beginning to emerge, grey mountains, above grey rocky plains; and though I crossed continent after continent I never came to a shore, because oceans and lakes and rivers were still lying underground somewhere or other.

You rarely met anyone in those days: there were so few of us! To survive with that ultraviolet you couldn't be too demanding. Above all the lack of atmosphere asserted itself in many ways; you take meteors for example: they fell like hail from all the points of space, because then we didn't have the stratosphere where nowadays they strike, as if on a roof, and disintegrate. Then there was the silence: no use shouting! Without any air to vibrate, we were all deaf and dumb. The temperature? There was nothing around to retain the Sun's heat: when night fell it was so cold you could freeze stiff. Fortunately, the Earth's crust warmed us from below, with all those molten minerals which were being compressed in the bowels of the planet. The nights were short (like the days: the Earth turned around faster); I slept huddled up to a very warm rock; the dry cold all around was pleasant. In other words, as far as the climate went, to tell you the truth, I wasn't so badly off.

Among the countless indispensable things we had to do without, the absence of colours – as you can imagine – was the least of our problems; even if we had known they existed, we would have considered them an unsuitable luxury. The only drawback was the strain on your eyes when you had to hunt for something or someone, because with everything equally colourless no form could be clearly distinguished from what was behind it or around it. You could barely make out a moving object: a meteor fragment as it rolled, or the serpentine yawning of a seismic chasm, or a lapillus being ejected from a volcano.

That day I was running through a kind of amphitheatre of porous, spongy rocks, all pierced with arches beyond which other arches opened; a very uneven terrain where the absence of colour was streaked by distinguishable concave shadows. And among the pillars of these colourless arches I saw a kind of colourless flash running swiftly, disappearing, then reappearing further on: two flattened glows that appeared and disappeared abruptly; I still hadn't realized what they were, but I was already in love and running, in pursuit of the eyes of Ayl.

I went into a sandy wasteland: I proceeded, sinking down among dunes which were always somehow different and yet almost the same. Depending on the point from which you looked at them, the crests of the dunes seemed the outlines of reclining bodies. There you could almost make out the form of an arm folded over a tender breast, with the palm open under a resting cheek; further on, a young foot with a slender big toe seemed to emerge. As I stopped to observe those possible analogies, a full minute went by before I realized that, before my eyes, I didn't have a sandy ridge but the object of my pursuit.

She was lying, colourless, overcome with sleep, on the colourless sand. I sat down nearby. It was the season – as I know now – when the ultraviolet era was approaching its end on our planet; a way of life about to finish was displaying its supreme peak of beauty. Nothing so beautiful had ever run over the Earth, as the creature I had before my eyes.

Ayl opened her eyes. She saw me. At first I believe she couldn't distinguish me – as had happened to me, with her – from the rest of that sandy world; then she seemed to recognize in me the unknown presence that had pursued her and she was frightened. But in the end she became aware of our common substance and there was a half-timid, half-smiling palpitation in the look she gave me, which caused me to emit a silent whimper of happiness.

I started conversing, all in gestures. 'Sand. Not-sand,' I said, first pointing to our surroundings, then to the two of us.

She nodded yes, she had understood.

'Rock. Not-rock,' I said, to continue that line of

reasoning. It was a period in which we didn't have many concepts at our disposal: to indicate what we two were, for example, what we had in common and what was different, was not an easy undertaking.

'I. You-not-I,' I tried to explain, with gestures.

She was irked.

'Yes. You-like-me, but only so much,' I corrected myself.

She was a bit reassured, but still suspicious.

'I, you, together, run run,' I tried to say.

She burst out laughing and ran off.

We ran along the crest of the volcanoes. In the noon greyness Ayl's flying hair and the tongues of flame that rose from the craters were mingled in a wan, identical fluttering of wings.

'Fire. Hair,' I said to her. 'Fire same hair.'

She seemed convinced.

'Not beautiful?' I asked.

'Beautiful,' she answered.

The Sun was already sinking into a whitish sunset. On a crag of opaque rocks, the rays, striking sidelong, made some of the rocks shine.

'Stones there not same. Beautiful, eh?' I said.

'No,' she answered, and looked away.

'Stones there beautiful, eh?' I insisted, pointing to the shiny grey of the stones.

'No.' She refused to look.

'To you, I, stones there!' I offered her.

'No. Stones here!' Ayl answered and grasped a handful of the opaque ones. But I had already run ahead.

I came back with the glistening stones I had collected, but I had to force her to take them.

'Beautiful!' I tried to persuade her.

'No!' she protested, but she looked at them; removed now from the Sun's reflections, they were opaque like the other stones; and only then did she say: 'Beautiful!'

Night fell, the first I had spent not embracing a rock, and perhaps for this reason it seemed cruelly shorter to me. The light tended at every moment to erase Ayl, to cast a doubt on her presence, but the darkness restored my certainty she was there.

The day returned, to paint the Earth with grey; and my gaze moved around and didn't see her. I let out a mute cry: 'Ayl! Why have you run off?' But she was in front of me and was looking for me, too; she couldn't see me and silently shouted: 'Qfwfq! Where are you?' Until our eyesight darkened, examining that sooty luminosity and recognizing the outline of an eyebrow, an elbow, a thigh.

Then I wanted to shower Ayl with presents, but nothing seemed to me worthy of her. I hunted for everything that was in some way detached from the uniform surface of the world, everything marked by a speckling, a stain.

But I was soon forced to realize that Ayl and I had different tastes, if not downright opposite ones: I was seeking a new world beyond the pallid patina that imprisoned everything, I examined every sign, every crack (to tell the truth something was beginning to change: in certain points the colourlessness seemed shot through with variegated flashes); instead, Ayl was a happy inhabitant of the silence that reigns where all vibration is excluded; for her anything that looked likely to break the absolute visual neutrality was a harsh discord; beauty began for her only where the greyness had extinguished even the remotest desire to be anything other than grey.

How could we understand each other? Nothing in the world that lay before our eyes was sufficient to express what we felt for each other, but while I was in a fury to wrest unknown vibrations from things, she wanted to reduce everything to the colourless beyond of their ultimate substance.

A meteorite crossed the sky, its trajectory passing in front of the Sun; its fluid and fiery envelope for an instant acted as a filter to the Sun's rays, and all of a sudden the world was immersed in a light never seen before. Purple chasms gaped at the foot of orange cliffs, and my violet hands pointed to the flaming green meteor while a thought for which words did not yet exist tried to burst from my throat:

'This for you! From me this for you, yes, yes, beautiful!'

At the same time I wheeled around, eager to see the new way Ayl would surely shine in the general transfiguration; but I didn't see her: as if in that sudden shattering of the colourless glaze, she had found a way to hide herself, to slip off among the crevices in the mosaic.

'Ayl! Don't be frightened, Ayl! Show yourself and look!'

But already the meteorite's arc had moved away from the Sun, and the Earth was reconquered by its perennial grey, now even greyer to my dazzled eyes, and indistinct, and opaque, and there was no Ayl.

She had really disappeared. I sought her through a long throbbing of days and nights. It was the era when the world was testing the forms it was later to assume: it tested them with the material it had available, even if it wasn't the most suitable, since it was understood that there was nothing definitive about the trials. Trees of smoke-coloured lava stretched out twisted branches from which hung thin leaves of slate. Butterflies of ash flying over clay meadows hovered above opaque crystal daisies. Ayl might be the colourless shadow swinging from a branch of the colourless forest or bending to pick grey mushrooms under grey clumps of bushes. A hundred times I thought I glimpsed her and a hundred times I thought I lost her again. From the wastelands I moved to the inhabited localities. At that time, sensing the changes that would take place, obscure builders were shaping premature images of a remote, possible future. I crossed a piled-up metropolis of stones; I went through a mountain pierced with passageways like an anchorite's retreat; I reached a port that opened upon a sea of mud; I entered a garden where, from sandy beds, tall menhirs rose into the sky.

The grey stone of the menhirs was covered with a pattern of barely indicated grey veins. I stopped. In the centre of this park, Ayl was playing with her female companions. They were tossing a quartz ball into the air and catching it.

Someone threw it too hard, the ball came within my reach, and I caught it. The others scattered to look for it; when I saw Ayl alone, I threw the ball into the air and caught it again. Ayl ran over; hiding, I threw the quartz ball, drawing Ayl further and further away. Finally I showed myself; she scolded me, then laughed; and so we went on, playing, through strange regions.

At that time the strata of the planet were laboriously trying to establish an equilibrium through a series of earthquakes. Every now and then the ground was shaken by one, and between Ayl and me crevasses opened across which we threw the quartz ball back and forth. These chasms gave the elements compressed in the heart of the

Earth an avenue of escape, and now we saw outcroppings of rock emerge, or fluid clouds, or boiling jets spurt up.

As I went on playing with Ayl, I noticed that a gassy layer had spread over the Earth's crust, like a low fog slowly rising. A moment before it had reached our ankles, and now we were in it up to our knees, then to our hips . . . At that sight, a shadow of uncertainty and fear grew in Ayl's eyes; I didn't want to alarm her, and so, as if nothing were happening, I went on with our game; but I, too, was anxious.

It was something never seen before: an immense fluid bubble was swelling around the Earth and completely enfolding it; soon it would cover us from head to foot, and who could say what the consequences would be?

I threw the ball to Ayl beyond a crack opening in the ground, but my throw proved inexplicably shorter than I had intended and the ball fell into the gap; the ball must have become suddenly very heavy; no, it was the crack that had suddenly yawned enormously, and now Ayl was far away, beyond a liquid, wavy expanse that had opened between us and was foaming against the shore of rocks, and I leaned from this shore, shouting: 'Ayl, Ayl!' and my voice, its sound, the very sound of my voice spread loudly, as I had never imagined it, and the waves rumbled still louder than my voice. In other words: it was all beyond understanding.

I put my hands to my deafened ears, and at the same moment I also felt the need to cover my nose and mouth, so as not to breathe the heady blend of oxygen and nitrogen that surrounded me, but strongest of all was the impulse to cover my eyes, which seemed ready to explode.

The liquid mass spread out at my feet had suddenly turned a new colour, which blinded me, and I exploded in an articulate cry which, a little later, took on a specific meaning: 'Ayl! The sea is blue!'

The great change so long awaited had finally taken place. On the Earth now there was air, and water. And over that newborn blue sea, the Sun – also coloured – was setting, an absolutely different and even more violent colour. So I was driven to go on with my senseless cries, like: 'How red the Sun is, Ayl! Ayl! How red!'

Night fell. Even the darkness was different. I ran looking for Ayl, emitting cries without rhyme or reason, to express what I saw: 'The stars are yellow, Ayl! Ayl!'

I didn't find her that night or the days and nights that followed. All around, the world poured out colours, constantly new, pink clouds gathered in violet cumuli which unleashed gilded lightning; after the storms long rainbows announced hues that still hadn't been seen, in all possible combinations. And chlorophyll was already beginning its progress: mosses and ferns grew green in the valleys where torrents ran. This was finally the setting worthy of Ayl's beauty; but she wasn't there! And without her all this varicoloured sumptuousness seemed useless to me, wasted.

I ran all over the Earth, I saw again the things I had once known grey, and I was still amazed at discovering fire was red, ice white, the sky pale blue, the earth brown, that rubies were ruby-coloured, and topazes the colour of topaz, and emeralds emerald. And Ayl? With all my imagination I couldn't picture how she would appear to my eyes.

I found the menhir garden, now green with trees and grasses. In murmuring pools red and blue and yellow fish were swimming. Ayl's friends were still leaping over the lawn, tossing the iridescent ball: but how changed they were! One was blonde with white skin, one brunette with olive skin, one brown-haired with pink skin, one had red hair and was dotted with countless, enchanting freckles.

'Ayl!' I cried. 'Where is she? Where is Ayl? What does she look like? Why isn't she with you?'

Her friends' lips were red, their teeth white, and their tongues and gums were pink. Pink, too, were the tips of their breasts. Their eyes were aquamarine blue, cherry-black, hazel and maroon.

'Why . . . Ayl . . .' they answered. 'She's gone . . . we don't know . . .' and they went back to their game.

I tried to imagine Ayl's hair and her skin, in every possible colour, but I couldn't picture her; and so, as I looked for her, I explored the surface of the globe.

'If she's not up here,' I thought, 'that means she must be below,' and at the first earthquake that came along, I flung myself into a chasm, down down into the bowels of the Earth.

'Ayl! Ayl!' I called in the darkness. 'Ayl, come see how beautiful it is outside!'

Hoarse, I fell silent. And at that moment Ayl's voice, soft, calm, answered me. 'Sssh. I'm here. Why are you shouting so much? What do you want?'

I couldn't see a thing. 'Ayl! Come outside with me. If you only knew . . . Outside . . .'

'I don't like it, outside . . .'

'But you, before . . .'

'Before was before. Now it's different. All that confusion has come.'

I lied. 'No, no. It was just a passing change of light. Like that time with the meteorite! It's over now. Everything is the way it used to be. Come, don't be afraid . . .' If she comes out, I thought, after the first moment of bewilderment, she'll become used to the colours, she'll be happy, and she'll understand that I lied for her own good.

'Really?'

'Why should I tell you stories? Come, let me take you outside.'

'No, you go ahead. I'll follow you.'

'But I'm impatient to see you again.'

'You'll see me only the way I like. Go ahead and don't turn around.'

The telluric shocks cleared the way for us. The strata of rock opened fanwise and we advanced through the gaps. I heard Ayl's light footsteps behind me. One more quake and we were outside. I ran along steps of basalt and granite which turned like the pages of a book: already, at the end, the breach that would lead us into the open air was tearing wide, already the Earth's crust was appearing beyond the gap, sunny and green, already the light was forcing its way towards us. There: now I would see the colours brighten also on Ayl's face . . . I turned to look at her.

I heard her scream as she drew back towards the darkness, my eyes still dazzled by the earlier light could make out nothing, then the rumble of the earthquake drowned everything, and a wall of rock suddenly rose, vertically, separating us.

'Ayl! Where are you? Try to come over to this side, quickly, before the rock settles!' And I ran along the wall looking for an opening, but the smooth, grey surface was compact, without a fissure.

An enormous chain of mountains had formed at that point. As I had been projected outwards, into the open, Ayl had remained beyond the rock wall, closed in the bowels of the Earth.

'Ayl! Where are you? Why aren't you out here?' and I looked around at the landscape that stretched away from my feet. Then, all of a sudden, those pea-green lawns where the first scarlet poppies were flowering, those canary-yellow fields which striped the tawny hills sloping down to a sea full of azure glints, all seemed so trivial to me, so banal, so false, so much in contrast with Ayl's person, with Ayl's world, with Ayl's idea of beauty, that I realized her place could never have been out here. And I realized, with grief and fear, that I had remained out here, that I would never again be able to escape those gilded and silvered gleams, those little clouds that turned from pale blue to pink, those green leaves that yellowed every autumn, and that Ayl's perfect world was lost for ever, so lost I couldn't even imagine it any more, and nothing was left that could remind me of it, even remotely, nothing except perhaps that cold wall of grey stone.

As Long as the Sun Lasts

Depending on their size, brightness and colour, stars have a varying evolution that can be classified according to the Hertzsprung-Russell diagram. Their life can be very brief (just a few million years, for the large blue stars) or they can follow such a slow course (ten billion years, for the smaller yellow stars) that before it brings them to old age their life can last (in the case of the reddest and smallest ones) for billions of millennia. For all of them there comes a moment when, once all their hydrogen has been burned, there is nothing more left for them to do except expand and cool down (turning into Red Giants) and from that point they embark on a series of thermonuclear reactions that will bring them swiftly to extinction. The Sun, a yellow star of medium power which has already been shining for four or five billion years, has in front of it a time that is at least just as long again, before it reaches that point.

It was precisely for that reason, to have a bit of a quieter life, that my grandfather came and settled here – *Qfwfq said* – after the last supernova explosion had flung them

38

once more into space: grandfather, grandmother, their children, grandchildren and great-grandchildren. The Sun was just at that stage condensing, a roundish, yellowish shape, along one arm of the galaxy, and it made a good impression on him, amidst all the other stars that were going around. 'Let's try a yellow one this time,' he said to his wife. 'If I've understood it right, the yellow ones are those that stay up longest without changing. And maybe in a short time from now a planetary system will form around it too.'

This idea of settling with all the family on one planet, maybe one of those with an atmosphere and beasties and plants, was one of Colonel Eggg's old ideas for when he would retire, after all those comings and goings amidst incandescent matter. Not that he suffered from the heat, my grandfather, and as for upheavals in temperature, he had had to get used to such things for some time now, after so many years of service; still, once you've got to a certain age, everyone starts to like a temperate climate around them.

My grandmother, though, immediately butted in: 'And why not on that other one? The bigger they are the more I trust them!' and she pointed to a Blue Giant.

'Are you mad, don't you know what that is? Don't you know about the blue ones? They burn so fast you don't even notice, and barely a couple of thousand millennia go by and you've already got to start packing!'

But you know how Grandma Ggge is: she's stayed young not just in her looks but also in her outlook, never happy with her lot, always craving change, no matter whether it's for better or worse, attracted by everything that is different. And to think that the bulk of the upheaval, in those hasty and panicky removals from one heavenly body to another, always landed on her shoulders, especially when there were small children around. 'It's as if she didn't remember from one move to the next,' Grandpa Eggg would say, letting off steam with us grandchildren. 'She never learns to calm down. I'm telling you, here, in the solar system, what can she complain about? I've been travelling all across galaxies for a long time now, so I've got a bit of experience, haven't I? And does my wife ever acknowledge that?'

This is the Colonel's obsession: he has had plenty to make him happy in his career, but he has never had this one satisfaction, the one he would like above all else: hearing his wife finally say, 'Yes, Eggg, you were spot on about this, I wouldn't have given tuppence for this Sun but you immediately managed to see that it was one of the most reliable and stable stars, one that wouldn't start to play tricks two minutes later, and you were also able to put us in the right position to get a place on the Earth, when it later took shape . . . and this Earth, with all its limits and defects, still offers good residential areas, and the kids have space to play and schools that are not too far away . . .' This is what the old Colonel would like his wife to tell him, indulging him just for once in his life. No chance. Instead, the minute she hears of some stellar system that works in a completely different way, for instance the varying luminosity of the 'RR Lyrae', her cravings begin: there life is probably more varied, you're more in the swing, whereas here we're stuck in this corner, in a dead end where nothing ever happens.

'And what is it you want to happen?' asked Eggg, appealing to all of us as witnesses. 'As if we didn't now know that it's the same story everywhere: hydrogen is transformed into helium, then come the usual tricks with beryllium and lithium, the incandescent layers collapsing on top of each other, then swelling like balloons and getting paler and paler until they collapse again . . . If we could only, while we're in the middle of it all, manage to enjoy the spectacle! But instead each time the great worry is not losing sight of the parcels and packages for the removal, and the kids crying, one daughter with inflamed eyes, a son-in-law whose denture is melting . . . The first to suffer from all this, everyone knows, is her, Ggge; she talks and talks, but when it comes to the actual event . . .'

Those early days were full of surprises for old Eggg too (he told us this so many times): the condensation of gas-clouds, the clash of atoms, matter clumping together and swelling and swelling until it ignites, and the sky swarming with white-hot bodies of every colour, each one seemingly different from all the others in diameter, temperature, density, in its way of contracting and dilating, and all those isotopes that nobody imagined existed, and those puffs and explosions, those magnetic fields . . . one unpredictable thing after the other. But now . . . all he needs is a glance and he's worked it all out: what star it is, what its spectrum is, how much it weighs, what it burns, whether it acts as a magnet or spews out stuff, and how far away the stuff that is spewed out stops, and how many light-years away there might be another star.

For him the expanse of void is like a cluster of tracks in a railway junction: these and no others are the gauges, points, diversions; you can take this or that route but you can't run in the middle or leap over the ballast. The same for the flow of time: every movement is slotted into a timetable which he knows by heart; he knows all the stops, delays, connections, deadlines, seasonal timetable variations. This had always been his dream for when he would retire from active service: to contemplate the ordered and regulated traffic that runs up and down the universe – like those pensioners who go to the station every day to see the trains arriving and departing – and to feel happy that he's no longer the one to be bounced around, laden with luggage and kids, amidst the indifferent comings and goings of those contraptions, each one whirling around on its own . . .

An ideal spot, then, from every point of view. In the four billion years they've been here, they've already settled in more or less, got to know a few people: folk who come and go, of course, that's the kind of place it is, but for Mrs Ggge, who loves variety so much, this ought to be a plus point. Now they have neighbours, on the same floor, Cavicchia they're called, who are really nice people: neighbours who help you out, pleasant neighbours you can rely on.

'I'd like to have seen you,' Eggg says to his wife, 'in the Clouds of Magellan: I bet you'd never have found such civilized people there!' (The thing is that Ggge, in her craving for other homes, even brings up extra-galactic constellations.)

But when someone has reached a certain age, there's no way you can change her ideas: if the Colonel hasn't managed it after so many years of marriage, he certainly won't manage it now. For instance, Ggge hears that their neighbours are leaving for Teramo. They're from the Abruzzi, the Cavicchias, and every year they go back to visit their relations. 'There,' says Ggge, 'everyone's leav-

43

ing and we're always stuck here. I've got my mother whom I've not been to see for billions of years!'

'When will you ever understand that it's not the same thing?' old Eggg protests.

My great-grandmother, you see, lives in the Andromeda Galaxy. Yes, at one stage she always travelled with her daughter and son-in-law, but right at the point when this clutch of galaxies started to form, they lost sight of each other: she went one way and they went the other. (Even today Ggge still blames the Colonel: 'You should have paid more attention,' she claims. And he replies: 'Oh yes, I had nothing else to do at that particular time!' This is all he says, so as not to point out that his mother-in-law, a wonderful woman, of course, but as a travelling companion, well, she was one of those people specially designed to complicate things, especially at moments of upheaval.)

The Andromeda Galaxy is straight up here, above our heads, but in between there are always a couple of billion light-years. For Ggge light-years seem like flea-jumps: she hasn't realized that space is a glue you get stuck in, just like time.

The other day, perhaps to cheer her up, Eggg said to her: 'Listen, Ggge, we won't necessarily stay here for ever. How many millennia have we been here? Four million? Well, let's say we must be halfway through our stay at the very least. Barely five million millennia will go by and the Sun will swell up until it swallows Mercury, Venus and Earth, and a series of cataclysms will start all over again, one after the other, at tremendous speed. Who knows where we'll land up? So, try to enjoy this small amount of peace that we have left.'

'Is that so?' she says, immediately interested. 'Well then, we mustn't be caught unawares. I'm going to start putting aside everything that won't go off and is not too cumbersome, so we can take it with us when the Sun explodes.'

And before the Colonel can stop her, she runs into the attic to see how many suitcases are there, what condition they're in, and to check they lock properly. (She claims to be thinking ahead by doing so: if you're flung out into space there is nothing worse than having to gather up the contents of suitcases that have been scattered in the midst of interstellar gas.)

'But what's your hurry?' Grandfather exclaims. 'We've still got several billion years in front of us, I told you!'

'Yes, but there are so many things to be done, Eggg, and I don't want to leave everything till the last minute. For example, I want to have some quince jam ready, in case we meet my sister Ddde, who's crazy about it: heaven knows how long it's been since she last tasted it, poor soul.'

'Your sister Ddde? Is she not the one on Sirius?'

I don't know how many there are in Grandma Ggge's

family, scattered here and there throughout every con-
stellation: and at every cataclysm she expects she'll meet
some of them. And in fact she's right: every time the
Colonel explodes into space, he finds himself in the
midst of newly acquired in-laws and cousins.

In short, there's no stopping her now: totally caught
up in her preparations, she thinks about nothing else,
and leaves the most urgent chores half done, because
'any moment now the Sun will finish'. Her husband is
beside himself at this: he had dreamed so much about
enjoying his retirement, allowing himself a rest amidst
the ongoing conflagrations, letting the heavenly cruci-
bles fry in their different fuels, sheltered from it all,
contemplating the passing of centuries as if it were a
uniform flow without any interruption, and now look
what's happened: just when they'd reached more or less
the exact mid-point of the holiday, Mrs Ggge starts getting him all worked up, with the suitcases flung open on
the beds, the drawers turned upside down, shirts piled
on top of each other; all the thousands of millions of
billions of hours and days and weeks and months that
he could have enjoyed as if the holiday were endless,
from now on he'll have to live through them as though
always on the point of leaving, just like when he was in
active service, always waiting to be transferred. He won't
be able to forget even for an instant that everything

around him is temporary, temporary but always repeated, a mosaic of protons, electrons, neutrons, that will fragment and come together again indefinitely, a soup that will be stirred until it cools or heats up: in short, this holiday in the most temperate planet in the solar system is completely ruined.

'What do you think, Eggg, some of the crockery if it's well wrapped up, I think we'll be able to take that with us without it breaking . . .'

'No, what are you thinking of, Ggge, with all the space it takes up, think of how many other things you've got to get in . . .' And he is forced to take part as well, to offer an opinion on the various problems, to share her endless impatience, to live life as though it were always the day before leaving.

I know what this old pensioner is now yearning for, he's told us clearly so many times: to be eliminated from it all once and for all, to let the stars perish and re-form and perish again a hundred thousand times, with Mrs Ggge and all his sisters-in-law in the middle chasing and embracing each other, and losing their hatboxes and umbrellas and finding them and losing them again, and him having nothing to do with any of it, staying at the bottom of matter that has been squeezed and chewed and spat out and is no use for anything . . . the White Dwarves!

Old Eggg is not one to talk just for the sake of it: he has a very precise plan in mind. You know those White Dwarves, those stars that are very dense and inert, the residue of the most violent explosions, searing hot from the white heat of the nuclei of metals that have been crushed and compressed inside each other? The ones that continue to go slowly round forgotten orbits, gradually turning into cold, opaque coffins for elements to be buried in? 'Let Ggge go, let her go,' Eggg chuckles, 'let her get carried away by the spurts of flying electrons. I'll wait here, until the Sun and everything that goes round it is reduced to a decrepit dwarf star; I'll dig myself a niche amidst the hardest atoms, I'll tolerate flames of every colour, as long as I can finally get to that dead end, that siding, as long as I can reach the shore that nobody ever leaves again.'

And he looks up with his eyes already as they will be when he is on his White Dwarf, and when the rotating of galaxies which light up and extinguish blue, yellow and red fires, and condense and dispel rainclouds and dustclouds, will no longer be the occasion for the usual conjugal bickering but something that exists, that is there, that is what it is, full stop.

And yet I believe that, at least in the early days of his stay on that deserted and forgotten star, he will want to continue mentally arguing with Ggge. It won't be easy for him to stop. I seem to see him, alone in the void, as he travels through the expanse of light years, but still quarrelling with his wife. That 'I told you so' and 'brilliant discovery' that accompanied the birth of the stars, the movement of galaxies, the cooling of planets, that 'you'll be happy now' and 'that's all you ever say' that marked every episode and phase and explosion of their quarrels and of heavenly cataclysms, that 'you always think you're right' and 'it's because you never listen to me' without which the history of the universe would not have for him any name or memory or flavour, that eternal conjugal bickering: if ever it should one day come to an end, what a feeling of desolation, what emptiness!

Implosion

'Over the last few years, quasars, Seyfert galaxies, BL Lacertae objects, or, more generally, active galactic nuclei, have been attracting the attention of astronomers because of the huge quantities of energy these bodies emit, at velocities of up to 10,000 kilometres per second. There are good reasons for supposing that the central driving force of the galaxy is a black hole of enormous mass' (L'Astronomia, no. 36). 'Active galactic nuclei may be fragments left unexploded by the Big Bang and engaged in a process exactly opposite to that which takes place in black holes, a process, that is, of explosive expansion involving the liberation of enormous quantities of energy ('white holes'). They could be explained as the exit extremities of a connecting link between two points in space-time (Einstein-Rosen's bridges), expelling material devoured by a black hole situated at the entrance extremity. According to this theory, a Seyfert galaxy a hundred million light years away may now be expelling gas sucked in by another part of the universe ten billion years ago. And it is even possible that a quasar ten billion light years away may have assumed the form *we see today by taking in material that reaches it from some point in the future, travelling through a black hole which, as far as we are concerned, formed only today' (Paolo Maffei, Monsters of the Sky, pp. 210–15).*

To explode or to implode – *said Qfwfq* – that is the question: whether 'tis nobler in the mind to expand one's energies in space without restraint, or to crush them into a dense inner concentration and, by ingesting, cherish them. To steal away, to vanish; no more; to hold within oneself every gleam, every ray, deny oneself every vent, suffocating in the depths of the soul the conflicts that so idly trouble it, give them their quietus; to hide oneself, to obliterate oneself: perchance to reawaken elsewhere, changed.

Changed . . . In what way changed? And the question, to explode or to implode: would one have to face it again? Absorbed by the vortex of this galaxy, does one pop up again in other times and other firmaments? Here sink away in cold silence, there express oneself in fiery shrieks of another tongue? Here soak up good and evil like a sponge in the shadow, there gush forth like a dazzling jet, to spray and spend and lose oneself? To what end then would the cycle repeat itself? I really don't know, I don't want to know, I don't want to think about it: here, now, my choice is made: I shall implode, as if this centripetal plunge might for ever save me from doubt and error, from the time of ephemeral change, from the slippery descent of before and after, bring me to a time of stability, still and smooth, enable me to achieve the one condition that is homogeneous and compact and definitive. You explode, if that's more to your taste, shoot yourselves all around in endless darts, be prodigal, spendthrift, reckless: I shall implode, collapse inside the abyss of myself, towards my buried centre, infinitely.

How long has it been since none of you has been able to imagine the life force except in terms of explosion? You have your reasons, I know. Your model is that of a universe born from a madcap explosion whose first splinters still hurtle unchecked and incandescent at the edge of space; your emblem is the exuberant kindling of supernovae flaunting the insolent youth of stars overloaded with energy; your favourite metaphor is the volcano, to show that even a mature and settled planet is always ready to break its bonds and burst forth. And the furnaces that flare in the furthest bounds of the heavens confirm your cult of universal conflagration; gases and particles almost as swift as light hurl themselves from vortex to centre of spiral galaxies, burst out into the lobes of elliptic galaxies, proclaim that the Big Bang still lives, the great Pan is not dead. No, I'm not deaf to your reasons; I could even join you. Go on!

Explode! Burst! Let the new world begin again, repeat its ever-renewed beginnings in a thunder of cannonfire, as in Napoleon's times . . . Wasn't it that age, by the way, with its elation at the revolutionary might of artillery fire that made us think of the explosion not just as harmful to people and property, but as a sign of birth, of genesis? Isn't it since then that passions, poetry and the ego have been seen as perpetual explosions? But if that's true, then so is its opposite; ever since that August when the mushroom rose over cities reduced to a layer of ash, an age was born in which the explosion is symbolic only of absolute negation. But that was something we already knew anyway, from the moment when, rising above the calendar of terrestrial chronicle, we enquired of the destiny of the universe, and the oracles of thermodynamics answered us: every existing form will break up in a blaze of heat; there is no entity can escape the irretrievable disorder of the corpuscles; time is a catastrophe, perpetual and irreversible.

Only a few old stars know how to get out of time; they are the open door to jump from a train headed for annihilation. At the limit of their decrepitude, shrunk to the size of Red Dwarfs or White Dwarfs, panting out the last glimmering gasp of the pulsar, compressed into neutron stars, here they are at last, light lost to the waste of the firmament, no more than the dark deletion of themselves, ready for the unstoppable collapse when everything, even light itself, falls inwards never to emerge again.

Praise be to the stars that implode. A new freedom opens up within them: annulled from space, exonerated from time, existing, at last, for themselves alone and no longer in relation to all the rest, perhaps only they can be sure they really exist. 'Black holes' is a derogatory nickname, dictated by envy: they are quite the opposite of holes, nothing could be fuller and heavier and denser and more compact, with a stubbornness to the way they sustain the gravity they bear within, as if clenching their fists, gritting their teeth, hunching their backs. Only on these terms can one save oneself from dissolving in overreaching extension, in Catherine wheels of effusion, exclamatory extroversion, effervescence and ebullition. Only in this way can one break through to a space–time where the implicit and the unexpressed don't lose their energy, where the pregnancy of meanings is not diluted, where discretion and keeping distance multiply the effectiveness of every action.

Don't distract yourselves fantasizing over the reckless behaviour of hypothetical quasi-stellar objects at the uncertain boundaries of the universe: it is here that you must turn your attention, to the centre of our galaxy, where all our calculations and instruments indicate the presence of a body of enormous mass that nevertheless remains invisible. Webs of radiation and gas, caught there perhaps since the time of the last implosions, show that there in the middle lies one of these so-called holes, spent as an old volcano. All that surrounds it, the wheel of planetary systems and constellations and the branches of the Milky Way, everything in our galaxy rests on the hub of this implosion sunk away into itself. That is my pole, my mirror, my secret home. It need fear no comparison with the furthest galaxies and their apparently explosive nuclei: there too what counts is what cannot be seen. Nothing comes out of there any more either, believe me: those impossibly fast flashes and whirls are just fuel to be crushed in the centripetal mortar, assimilated into the other mode of being, my own.

Sometimes, of course, I do seem to hear a voice from the furthest galaxies: 'It's me, Qfwfq, I am yourself exploding as you implode: I'm splashing out, expressing myself, spreading myself about, communicating, realizing all the potential I have; I really exist, not like you, introverted, reticent, egocentric, fused in an immutable self . . .'

Then I'm overwhelmed by the fear that even beyond the barrier of gravitational collapse time continues to flow: a different time, with no relation to the time left on this side, but speeding similarly headlong on a road with no return. In that case the implosion I've leaped into would be just a lull I've been granted, a respite before the fate I cannot escape.

Something like a dream, or a memory, goes through my mind: Qfwfq is fleeing the catastrophe of time, he finds an escape route through which to elude his destiny, he rushes through the gap, he is sure he has reached safety, from a chink in his refuge he watches how the events he has escaped gather pace, pities, from a distance, those who are overwhelmed, until, yes, he seems to recognize one of them, yes, it's Qfwfq, it's Qfwfq who beneath Qfwfq's very eyes is experiencing that same catastrophe of before or after, Qfwfq who in the moment he perishes sees Qfwfq save himself, but without saving him. 'Qfwfq, save yourself!' cries Qfwfq, but is it the imploding Qfwfq who wants to save the exploding Qfwfq or vice versa? No Qfwfq can save any exploding Qfwfqs from the conflagration, as they in turn can't pull back the other Qfwfqs from their unstoppable implosion. Any way time runs it leads to disaster whether in one direction or its opposite and the intersecting of those directions does not form a network of rails governed by points and exits, but a tangle, a knot . . .

I know I mustn't listen to voices, nor give credit to visions or nightmares. I go on digging my hole, in my mole's burrow.